# MICHELLE

---

## THE MERMAIDS OF ELDORIS, BOOK 1

### PJ RYAN

PJRYANBOOKS.COM

# ONE

Under the sea, things rarely moved fast. Fish glided through the water. The currents flowed peacefully. Mermaids swam in and out of the rock formations that sprouted up from the sand in the deepest water.

To Michelle, it was wonderful—until it was time for a crowning. Then everything moved so fast that Michelle could barely keep up with it. Normally she was excited for the adventure and festivities, but this time was different.

Michelle smoothed down the scarf that her sister had just draped around her shoulders. It was as blue as the water all around her.

"I'm sorry, I couldn't find the pink one." Arianna swam around behind her and fixed a twist in the scarf. "I think this one is perfect, though."

"It's fine." Michelle's heart pounded. She wished she wasn't wearing any scarf at all.

"Aren't you excited?" Arianna twisted her finger through her sister's hair. "You're going to get your crown!"

"Sure." Michelle smiled as she looked up at her sister. "It'll be great."

"She doesn't sound excited." Her other sister, Harriet, put her hands on her hips. "Michelle, have you practiced your song?"

"Yes, yes, I have." Michelle crossed her fingers. She hadn't gotten past the first part of the melody she was meant to sing at the crowning.

"Good job." Arianna smiled.

"She's lying." Harriet crossed her arms. "Michelle, you can't mess this up. Father and Mother will be so upset if you do."

"She'll do fine. Leave her alone!" Arianna waved her hand through the water and sent a ripple of bubbles straight at Harriet's face.

"Fine, let her lie to you. The truth will come out soon enough." Harriet flicked her tail through the water and sent a ripple of water back at Arianna as she left.

"Don't let her get to you. I'm sure you'll do just fine." Arianna smiled as she looked at her little sister. "Tomorrow is a special day for you. Smile."

"I don't want to smile." Michelle flicked her tail and pulled away from her sister. "I don't think I want to do this."

"Michelle, you don't have a choice." Arianna stared at her. "You're a princess and you must be crowned."

"And then what?" She shook her head. "I won't be able to swim off on my own anymore. I won't be able to play games with Trina and Kira. I'll just have to stay inside the palace grounds."

"It's for your safety." Arianna frowned. "Being a princess comes with many important jobs, but it also puts you at risk. You know that Father has enemies in the sea that would like to see someone else be king. They'd stop at nothing to make that happen."

"But I'm not afraid." Michelle sighed. "I'm more afraid of being stuck in one place than I'll ever be of Father's enemies. I mean, have you ever actually seen any of them?" She crossed her arms as she stared at her sister. "I know we've all heard the stories since we were babies, but have you ever seen one of these scary creatures that Father claims are out there?"

"No, I haven't."

"Because they're not real!"

"Because Father keeps us safe!" Arianna frowned. "You're too young to know better. There are horrible creatures out there and the very worst are a kind you never want to meet—a kind that will put you in a cage and never set you free. Humans."

"They are a myth!" Michelle laughed. "Even Ellen says so."

"Ellen thinks she knows a lot about everything, but she's never been off the palace grounds." Arianna flicked her tail sharply in the water, sharp enough to create a shower of tiny bubbles. "Humans are real. I know they are and Father does too. You'd better not let him hear you talking like this."

"It's silly to think so." Michelle gazed off through the endless water all around her. "To think that there is an entire world above the water. A place where people walk instead of swim and breathe through their noses instead of gills. It doesn't make much sense, does it, Arianna?"

"If Father says it's true, then I know it's true." Arianna looked into her sister's eyes. "You will be at your crowning tomorrow, Michelle, and you'll do as Father says."

"Don't I have any choice? What if I don't want to be a princess? What if I don't want to be safe?" She turned away from her sister.

"Well, we all love you too much not to keep you safe." Arianna gave her a warm hug. "You're just nervous. You'll do fine. Don't let Harriet worry you. I'll be back to check on you later." Arianna swam off through the water in the direction of the main palace.

The palace grounds stretched as far as Michelle could see.

The rocks towered up through the water, covered in coral and sea life. It was a beautiful home.

But when Michelle looked at it, all she saw was a prison. Once she was crowned, she would be expected to follow the rules of every princess. And Michelle had never been good at following rules.

As she swam away from the palace, she wondered what it would be like to explore—to really explore. To swim further than she'd ever swam before.

She often listened to the stories of older mermaids. They would tell tales of other places in the sea, places where the water was warmer or colder, places where the sand was a different color and the sea plants glowed.

All of it sparked her curiosity. All of it made her want to see it for herself.

But that was not her destiny.

Her destiny was to be one of the three princesses of Eldoris, a vast expanse that her father ruled over.

It was a beautiful and peaceful place. But could it ever be enough for her?

# TWO

Michelle plucked at the sand, then dug her fingers into it. Usually playing with the sand helped her to relax. Today, it didn't help much. Each moment that passed brought her closer to the big day.

"There you are!" Trina swooped down through the water and landed with a puff of sand right beside her. "I've been looking for you everywhere!"

"I told you she'd be here." Kira plopped down on the other side of Michelle. "She always hides out near the caves when she's upset."

"I do?" Michelle's eyes widened.

"You do." Kira crossed her arms over her knees and looked at Michelle. "It's the crowning, isn't it?"

"It is." Michelle frowned and dug her fingers into the sand again.

"Why don't we go hunt some jellyfish?" Trina nudged her with her elbow. "That always makes you feel better."

"That does sound like fun." Michelle smiled at her friend. "But I don't have my net with me."

"I do." Trina snapped her fingers and a net appeared in her hand. "You can use mine."

"There's no time to catch jellyfish! Michelle needs to get ready for her crowning." Kira crossed her arms.

"No way!" Trina grinned. "She needs to have nonstop fun! After the crowning, she'll have all those rules to follow. But until tomorrow, she's still free!"

"Exactly." Michelle looked up at her friends. "I do want to have fun. It might be the last fun I ever have."

"Don't think that way." Kira hugged her. "Being a princess is very special. Trina and I will never be princesses. And you'll always be safe inside the palace. The guards will protect you. You'll get to learn so much."

"I know all those things." Michelle frowned. "But what if I don't want to be safe? What if I want to see everything that's out there?" She looked off through the expanse of water. "There's so much more, don't you think? So much that we've never seen before?"

"I don't know. I kind of like it here." Kira whispered. "I know some of the things that are out there. Sharks." She shivered. "Giant squids." She closed her eyes tight. "And worst of all —lobsters!"

"Lobsters are worst of all?" Trina giggled. "What's so bad about lobsters? I would love to have one as a pet!"

"Ah! You're nuts!" Kira covered her face. "Their googly eyes and their clacking claws? How terrible!"

"Clacking claws?" Trina snapped her teeth together. "Like that? Does it sound like that?" She snapped her teeth again.

"Trina!" Kira gasped and covered her ears.

"Alright, alright!" Michelle laughed. "I know there are probably some scary things out there. But for every scary thing, I'll bet there are wonderful things too." She sighed and looked back out through the water. "Is it so wrong that I want to find out?"

"It's not wrong." Trina frowned, then hugged Michelle. "But it might not be possible."

"It's just not fair." Michelle swam up out of the sand. She swirled her tail through the water with a sharp snap. "Maybe I just don't want to be a princess!"

"Only you wouldn't want to be a princess." Kira looked back toward the coral palace. "I'd love to live inside the palace. It's sure better than mining for sea stones. That's the future I have."

"But it doesn't have to be. You could explore if you wanted to." Michelle swooped down to her. "You could go anywhere, see everything!"

"Be eaten by a shark! Remember?" Kira rolled her eyes. "No thanks. I'd take a nice fluffy bed in the palace any day."

"I wish we could switch places." Michelle crossed her arms. "Then we would both be happy."

"But we can't." Kira looked into her eyes. "Michelle, you're my best friend. I want you to be happy, but, if you keep dreaming like this, you never will be. The truth is, you are a princess and you are going to be crowned and then you will live in the palace. It's time you just got used to it. Just like the rest of us have to get used to the futures we have. It's just the way it is. It's the way it has to be."

"Why?" Michelle punched the water in front of her. "Why does it have to be that way?"

"It's how it's always been." Trina shrugged. "I don't know why."

"Look!" She pointed at the coral that grew on a piece of rock that jutted out of the sand. "Do you see that coral?"

"Yes." Trina looked at the coral. "What about it?"

"When I first came here, it was just a tiny dot. But over time it's gotten bigger and bigger. Just like me. Just like you and Kira. The ocean doesn't stay the same and neither do we, so why do the rules have to always stay the same?" She snapped her tail. "I'm going to find out!"

As she swam through the water she barely heard Kira call out to her.

"Michelle, don't upset your mother!"

Michelle ignored the warning and swam as swiftly as she could back toward the palace. She often raced her friends and most of the time she won. She loved to swim fast. But in the palace, there was nowhere to swim fast without running into rock.

In the palace she would be stuck in the same places forever.

# THREE

Michelle burst through the seaweed that covered the entrance to the throne room. It was the same place she would receive her crown the next day. The walls sparkled with sea stones of all different colors.

Two large shells sat in the center of the room, each lined with soft sand. Her mother perched on one, her tail curled up alongside of her. Her head rested on her hand as she gazed up through the open hole in the top of the throne room.

Schools of fish swam by, their silver scales flickering in the beams of light that filtered down through the water.

"Mother!" Michelle swam up to her. "I have to talk to you!"

"Not now, Michelle." Her mother waved her hand. "I'm resting. I need to be ready for the crowning tomorrow."

"But Mother, that's what I need to talk to you about." Michelle swam closer. Her mother's long hair flowed through the water. In Michelle's mind, she looked like a pearl—perfect and impossible to get to.

"What is it?" Her mother finally looked at her. "Oh, Michelle, what have you done to your hair? Your sisters will have to fix it before tomorrow."

"Please, Mother, I need to know—will I have to stay in the palace forever after I'm crowned?"

"You already know that, dear." Her mother sat up and looked at her. "It's so sweet that you're nervous. Come up here with me." She patted the soft sand in her shell.

"Mother, I'm not nervous." Michelle curled up beside her. "Is it really forever? Don't you ever leave the palace?"

"It is forever." Her mother trailed her fingers through her hair. "It's the only way to make sure that we are all safe."

"But why is it a rule?" Michelle frowned. "Who decided it the first time?"

"Your grandfather."

"My grandfather?" Michelle stared at her mother. "But I don't have a grandfather."

"You did." Her mother draped her arm around her shoulder. "He knew how dangerous the ocean was. He knew better than anyone. He made the rule to keep the royal family safe, because that's the only way we can keep the rest of the mermaids safe. There is so much danger out there."

"Sharks? Mother, most sharks don't want to hurt us. If we leave them alone, they leave us alone. The really scary creatures live in the deep dark sea, not here, where the light shines through." She looked up through the hole in the ceiling. "Is there really so much to be afraid of?"

"Yes, my darling." Her mother kissed the top of her head. "So much that we know about and even more that we don't. But don't worry. After tomorrow, you'll never have to be afraid. You will be safe in the palace with the rest of us and one day you will have a daughter whom you will keep safe as well."

"No!" Michelle pulled away from her mother. "I won't! I won't ever make her stay in one place."

"Michelle." Her mother swam toward her. "You will get used to it. You'll see how wise it is."

"No, I won't!" She swam away from her. "I don't want to be a princess, Mother! I don't want to be stuck in this palace forever! I don't care what Grandfather said!"

"Do not speak that way about him!" her mother shouted, which made the water all around her ripple. The waves carried swiftly in all directions and slammed into the palace walls, which made the entire palace tremble. "Your grandfather was a wonderful, wise man!"

"Then what happened to him?" Michelle shivered as she watched her mother swim toward her. It wasn't often that she saw her mother get angry, but when she did, it scared her. It scared everyone who saw it. "If the palace keeps us all safe, then what happened to Grandfather?"

"He broke his rule. He went out into the ocean—into the beyond—and he never came back!" The walls shook again.

Her mother closed her eyes. She swayed back and forth in the water. When she spoke again, her voice was softer.

"I'm sorry, Michelle, but you are a princess. You are part of this family. Being part of this family means that it is your job to protect all the mermaids, and the only way that you can do that is to keep yourself safe. It may seem unfair now, but one day you will understand." She touched her daughter's cheek. "I love you, but these are the rules, and they're not going to change. Tomorrow you will be crowned and you will become a protector of all the mermaids—of all your friends and of all the beings that live in our world. Don't you think that's something to be proud of?"

"I'm sure it is." Michelle looked down at the rock floor beneath her. "But it's not what I want." She looked back up at her mother. "I just want to explore."

"Never." Her mother stared hard into her eyes. "Do you hear me, Michelle? You will never explore. It's time you put those silly ideas out of your head. It's time you grew up."

"Mother, please—"

"No!" The walls shook again, this time so hard that a few of the sea stones tumbled out of the rock.

"You will stay in your shell until it's time for the crowning." Her mother pointed to the seaweed door. "Go! Now!"

Her voice was so powerful that the force of it carrying through the water pushed Michelle back through the door. She grabbed the rock wall just as she would have passed through it.

"Mother?" Her voice softened.

"Go, Michelle!" Her mother turned away from her.

"I'm sorry about Grandfather," she whispered. "You must have been so sad when you lost him."

"Yes, Michelle. Yes, I was." She swam back toward her shell and curled up again. She looked back at the open spot in the ceiling.

Michelle watched as the light that filtered through the water flickered against her mother's skin. She looked like a jewel, like the sea stones in the wall.

Maybe her mother was right about everything.

# FOUR

That night as Michelle tried to sleep, she kept seeing the flickering on her mother's skin. It was just a trick of light and the fish swimming by, but to her it seemed like so much more.

Her mother spent all her time cooped up in the palace. She claimed to be happy, but she never looked happy to Michelle. In fact, most of the time, Michelle thought she looked pretty sad.

Would that be her one day as her mother said? Would she have the same talk with her own daughter? She shivered at the thought. Yes, that was a long time in the future, but that future would be set in stone the next day.

As her thoughts continued to swirl, she swam out of bed. She looked out through a small window in the stone wall of her room and saw a distant glow.

What was it? A shiny creature? A pocket of moonlight that managed to make its way through the water?

She had no idea, and if she was crowned, she never would.

Her heart pounded as she made a decision. She gathered a few things around her room, snapped her fingers, and watched the objects disappear. They would travel with her and be at her fingertips when she needed them.

She looked back out the window. The glow had faded, but her choice stayed the same.

When everyone gathered for the crowning the next day, there would be one mermaid missing. She just had to get past her mother.

As she crept out of her room, she peered down the corridor in search of anyone who might catch her. For a moment, she thought about going right back to her shell.

There were a million things to be afraid of, things she knew about and things she could never imagine. Yes, it was scary. But it could also be amazing. She had to know what was out there, even if it meant leaving the only world she knew behind.

After one last moment of hesitation, she swam forward and right out into the open water. It wouldn't be long before she was missed. She had to get as far as she could, otherwise the guards would find her.

As she reached the edge of the palace grounds, she looked back over her shoulder. She thought about her parents and her sisters. Her heart ached when she thought of leaving Trina and Kira behind. They had all been best friends since they were tiny mermaids. She would miss them the most.

Still, she swam forward. She had never heard of anyone leaving the safety of the mermaid world. But she knew that one merman had. Her grandfather. But he hadn't come back either.

Was that because he'd gotten lost? Encountered a terrible danger? Or did he come across something too wonderful to swim away from?

The further she swam, the more certain she became that she would not turn back. Adventure awaited her!

She charged through the water in the direction of the glow that she'd seen. Maybe it was nothing more than some glowing coral, but maybe—maybe it was to be her first adventure.

She swam until she couldn't see the palace anymore. As the

water grew deeper and darker, her heart pounded faster. She'd never been so far away from home before.

Exhausted from swimming so fast, she stretched out on a large flat rock. She knew she had to keep moving, but a little rest couldn't hurt. She closed her eyes and felt the water flow over her skin.

When she opened her eyes again, she saw a squid making its way toward her. Her eyes widened. Squids were not allowed past the boundaries of the mermaid world. The guards made sure of it. She had always been told they were quite dangerous.

It was too late to hide. It swam closer and closer.

She remained very still. Maybe the squid would think she was part of the rock.

"Why, hello there." The squid's long tentacles drifted through the water in her direction.

He wasn't the biggest squid she'd ever seen, but he certainly wasn't the smallest. He was bigger than she was. With her focus on the creature in front of her, she almost forgot about the darkness all around her and the many other creatures that could sneak up behind her.

"H-hello."

"Are you lost?" The squid swam a little closer.

"No." She shivered. "Well, I don't actually know where I am, but I'm not lost."

"That seems impossible." The squid smiled. "I'll take you back to the Coral Palace."

"No." She drew back. "I don't want to go back."

"What do you mean?" He swung his tentacles through the water. "It's not safe for you to be out here. I'll take you back right now."

"No!" She backed up again until she bumped into the rock she had been lying on. "I'm not going back."

"You've run away?" He sank down to the sand. "How brave!

How foolish!" He crept closer to her along the sand. "All alone in the deep? Why, there are so many dangers."

"Stay back!" Michelle swam up into the water away from him.

"Frightened, are you?" He swung his long tentacles through the water, which stirred it up.

"Please stop that!" Michelle twirled in the fast current he'd created. As she spun around, she realized she might have made a terrible mistake.

# FIVE

"Now!" someone shouted as Michelle continued to spin.

Through the bubbles and sloshing water, she made out two mermaids as they tangled thick sea grass around the squid's arms.

Michelle finally stopped spinning. Still dizzy, she swam toward the two mermaids.

"Let me go!" The squid tried to get free of the grass.

"No way!" Trina crossed her arms. "You shouldn't have been messing with our friend!"

"Michelle, are you okay?" Kira swam over to her.

"I think so." Michelle stared at them both. "How did you find me?"

"We followed you." Trina smiled. "We saw you sneak out."

"You did? But I was so careful." Michelle frowned.

"We were going to surprise you and take you out for a swim with the jellyfish before your crowning. But we saw you sneak out, so we thought we should follow you." Kira looked into her eyes. "Is what he said true? Were you really going to run away?"

"Not going to. I did." Michelle swam closer to her friends. "I don't want to be a princess. I just want to be free."

"A princess?" The squid wiggled in the grass. "Dear me, dear me, you shouldn't be out here all alone! I was only going to take you back! Now I *must* take you back—right this second!" He broke free of the grass. "Let's go—and hurry!"

"No, no, no!" Michelle ducked under his swinging arms. "I won't go back, not ever!"

"Not ever?" Kira stared at her. "What about your sisters and your parents?"

"What about us?" Trina grabbed Michelle's hand.

"I will miss you all so much, but once that crown is placed on my head, I won't ever be free again. I have to do what my heart tells me to. I have to explore!" She flipped her tail through the water. "I can't expect you to understand, but you can't stop me!"

"We don't want to stop you." Trina swam around her. "But if you're going to go, we're going with you! Right, Kira?"

"Run away?" Kira shook her head. "I'm not sure that's such a good idea."

"It isn't." The squid swam in a slow circle around the three of them. "The open sea is a dangerous place. It's nowhere for three mermaids to wander."

"As long as we stick together, we'll be fine." Trina wrapped her arm around Michelle's shoulder. "What do you say, Kira? Are you going back or are you coming on an adventure with us?"

"You two should go home." Michelle frowned. "I don't want you to get in trouble because of me."

"No way." Kira crossed her arms. "Trina is right. If you're going, we're going."

"This is a terrible idea." The squid sank down into the sand. "I warned you. Remember that."

"Don't worry about him." Trina tipped her head toward the open water. "Let's go see what we can find."

"Are you sure?" Michelle glanced between her friends. "If we get caught, we'll all be in a lot of trouble."

"We're sure." Kira linked her arm through Michelle's. "You lead the way, adventurer!"

"Okay!" Michelle grinned.

As she began to swim off, she looked back once over her shoulder. The squid watched her from his perch in the sand. He didn't try to stop them or hurt them. Maybe he had been telling the truth, that he didn't want to cause them harm, that he just wanted to protect them. But she didn't want to be protected.

She swam swiftly through the water, with her friends just behind her. Now that she wasn't alone, she was even more excited to see what the open sea might have in store for her.

"Catch!" Trina called out as she tossed a round shell through the water.

"Got it!" Kira caught the shell, then tossed it into the water toward Michelle.

Michelle gave it a hard whack with her tail and the shell sailed through the water ahead of them.

"I'm getting it!" Kira laughed as she blasted past Michelle and hit the shell back toward her just before it could fall into the sand.

"Got it!" Michelle laughed and lunged for it.

"No, you don't!" Trina swooped in front of her and knocked the shell back toward Kira.

Kira swam backwards as she tried to catch it. "Got it, got it, got it!" she shrieked.

"Kira!" Michelle's eyes widened as she watched a dark cloud form in the water just behind Kira.

"Kira! Come back!" Trina shouted.

"Got it!" Kira laughed as she caught the shell in her hands. Then she looked at her friends. "What? What is it?"

"Don't move!" Michelle swam slowly toward her.

"Why not?" Kira looked over her shoulder and saw nothing but inky darkness. "Oh no!" She closed her mouth tight.

Maybe the squid they had met not long before was friendly, but this creature that had spewed its ink out into the water was not.

"Kira! Swim away from it!" Michelle called out to her.

"I'm trying!" Kira tried to swim forward, but she couldn't. Something had wrapped around her, though she couldn't see what it was. "It's like I'm tangled in something!"

"We have to save her!" Michelle swam forward but stopped as the ink drifted toward her.

"We can't reach her." Trina frowned. "There has to be another way to get her out of there!"

"We'll just have to go in and get her." Michelle swam forward again, determined to get through the ink before it could poison her.

"No, Michelle!" Trina grabbed her arm and pulled her back. "You can't, you'll never make it out."

"Oh no, here comes the octopus!" Michelle's eyes widened as she saw a giant figure begin to form in the cloud of ink.

# SIX

"Coming through! Excuse me, please!" A large lobster scuttled across the sand in Kira's direction.

"Wait! Don't go over there!" Michelle pointed to the cloud of ink.

"No worries! That can't hurt me!" He charged toward Kira with his claws high in the air.

"Oh no, no, no!" Kira wriggled but she didn't swim forward.

"Be still!" the lobster barked. Then he began clacking his claws at Kira.

"Don't! Yikes! He's going to cut me to bits!" Kira cried out.

"Don't hurt her!" Michelle swam toward the lobster.

"Stop snapping at her!" Trina swam after Michelle.

"Be free!" The lobster chuckled and waved his claws through the air.

"What?" Kira wriggled again, but this time she swam forward. "I'm free!" She swam as fast as she could.

Michelle and Trina each hooked an arm through Kira's and they swam as fast as they could with her.

Although Michelle didn't dare to look back, she could feel the giant presence of the octopus just behind her. She'd known this would be a risk when she set off on her adventure, but now that it was real, she was very scared.

"Those rocks!" She pointed to a pile of large rocks ahead of them. "We should be able to fit in those cracks and the octopus won't be able to reach us there."

"Yes, let's do it!" Trina swam through the slender opening first.

Kira followed after her.

Michelle was the last to try to get through. When she tried to squeeze past, she got her arm pinned up against her side. As she tried to wriggle free, she found it was impossible.

"I'm stuck!" She reached her free hand out to Kira and Trina.

"We'll get you out!" Kira tugged as hard as she could.

"It's okay, Michelle, we've got you!" Trina tugged too.

"It's not working." Michelle frowned. "I'm really stuck." She tried not to panic as she imagined the octopus swimming up behind her.

"Can you back out?" Kira gave her a firm shove.

Michelle moved a tiny bit, but not enough to get free.

"I'm not getting anywhere!" Michelle's heart pounded. She felt something slippery glide along her tail. "Oh no!" She shivered. "I think the octopus has me!"

"No, he's not getting you!" Kira wrapped her arm around Michelle's.

Trina did the same. "Michelle, we're going to get you out!"

Michelle's teeth chattered with fear as the slimy touch crawled up along her back. She did her best not to scream as it crawled down along her pinned arm.

"Maybe he can't get me out either! Maybe when he sees I'm stuck, he'll lose interest!" She hoped that was the case but as she felt the slimy touch run up and down along her arm, she doubted that he would give up.

"Michelle!" Kira shrieked. "There's something on your arm and it's not an octopus!"

"What?" Michelle twisted her head, but no matter how hard she tried, she couldn't see what was on her arm.

"It's a sea slug!" Trina giggled. "Aw, and it's so cute!"

"A what?" Michelle wriggled in fear. When she did, her arm came free and she was able to swim forward between the rocks. She swam so fast that she crashed right into Trina.

"She must have left a slime trail on your arm." Trina helped steady Michelle as she peered at the sea slug still stuck to Michelle's arm.

"It's not polite to call it slime." The sea slug rippled her long body, then crawled off of Michelle's arm and onto the back of Trina's hand. "Carlos said you might need some help."

"The coast is clear!" Carlos, the lobster, scuttled between the rocks. "That pesky octopus found better things to do!"

"Ah! Get it away from me!" Kira shrieked as she swam away from the lobster.

"Kira!" Michelle crossed her arms. "Carlos saved your life!"

"Oh, right—well—" She cleared her throat and swam a little closer. "He's still a lobster! Look at those claws!"

"Without these claws, I would never have been able to set you free." Carlos waved them through the water. "Thank you for all your help, Bea!"

"Always happy to help a mermaid." The sea slug crawled up along Trina's arm. "You three are far from home. Are you lost?"

Michelle noticed a flicker of something stuck to Carlos's claw. "What's this?" She swam over to him.

"We're exploring." Trina peered at the sea slug. "You are such a beautiful creature!"

"Thank you." Bea bowed to Trina. "So are you!"

"Carlos, what's stuck to your claw?" Michelle picked at the nearly invisible thread that floated off the end of Carlos's claw.

"Ah, this." He glared at it. "They call it fishing line."

"They?" She tugged at the fishing line until she managed to pull it free. "It's so strong, but so thin and I can barely see it!"

"That's what makes it so dangerous." Carlos frowned as the other mermaids gathered close to him. "I've found it wrapped around even the greatest of creatures. They use so much of it that it's everywhere in the sea."

"They?" Michelle frowned. "You keep saying they. What kind of magnificent creature could invent something like this?"

"They are the humans." Carlos stared at each of them in turn. "And there is nothing magnificent about them."

"Humans?" Michelle narrowed her eyes. "What are those? Some kind of shark?" She had heard her sisters mention the creatures, but she never really believed them at all.

"Actually, they look more like you." He tugged lightly at Michelle's hair with his claw. "They have hair like yours, two eyes, a nose, and a mouth—not too different from yours." He pointed to her long tail. "But instead of a tail, they have two legs."

"Legs?" Kira squeaked.

"Legs." He nodded.

"It must be hard for them to swim with those." Michelle frowned as she looked at the fishing line.

"Maybe, but it is very easy for them to walk on them." He clacked his claws. "They are land creatures."

"What?" Trina took the fishing line from Michelle to have a look. "What's a land creature?"

"They live outside the water." Carlos looked at them. "Hasn't anyone told you about the other world?"

# SEVEN

"He's teasing us!" Kira rolled her eyes. "He's making up these stories to try to scare us!"

"I'm doing no such thing!" Carlos waved his claws through the water. "I can't believe that you've never been told!"

"Carlos, you shouldn't have told them either." Bea crawled off of Trina's arm and onto one of the large rocks. "The mermaids have new laws now. They are not to speak of such things."

"Not to speak of it?" Carlos shook his head. "But that's ridiculous! Mermaids must know about the dangers of the other world! They must know in order to be safe!"

"Tell me." Michelle swam toward him. "I want to know everything!"

"Don't believe him, Michelle!" Kira crossed her arms. "If there was another world, your mother and father would have told us. Our king and queen would never lie to us!"

"King and queen." Carlos floated back away from Michelle. "You're a princess?"

"I haven't been crowned yet." Michelle waved her hand. "Never mind that, tell me about this other world!"

"I've already said too much." He looked over at Bea. "I didn't know!"

"Just zip your lips now!" Bea huffed. "You've caused enough trouble! We need to get these three home right away, before the guards come looking for them!"

"No, we're not going back." Michelle swam away from the two creatures.

"Michelle, maybe we should," Kira whispered. "Maybe it's best."

"Even if we wanted to go back, I have no idea where home is." Trina swam over to Michelle. "We've come this far and we really can't turn back."

"They can take us!" Kira pointed to the lobster and the sea slug. "Can't you?"

"Not if you don't know the way." Carlos hung his head. "I don't know exactly where the mermaid world is."

"Neither do I." Bea slid across the rock. "You three are truly lost now."

"I'm sorry that I got the two of you into this." Michelle floated down to the sand. "I wouldn't ever want either one of you to be in danger. Now we're lost and there's no way for us to get back home."

"It's not your fault." Trina settled in the sand next to her. "We knew what we were getting into when we followed you. Didn't we, Kira?"

"Uh, mostly." She edged around the lobster, then settled on the other side of Michelle. "This is adventure, isn't it? It doesn't always go the way you expect it to."

"I don't know what I thought I would find out here." Michelle looked out at the water. "Something magical, I guess. Something wonderful, maybe."

"You found me!" Carlos clacked his claws. "It doesn't get much better than that, does it?" He scuttled along the sand.

26

"True." Michelle laughed. "You are quite a hero, Carlos."

"I learned it from the best." He pointed a claw at Michelle. "A great adventurer, not unlike yourself. In fact, he's a mermaid too."

"A mermaid?" She stared at the lobster. "What do you mean? You've met another mermaid on an adventure?"

"Eh, is it merman?" He tipped his head from side to side. "I wasn't sure."

"Yes, actually, that's right." Michelle met his eyes. "That man you met—I think he might have been my grandfather." She swooped through the water closer to Carlos. "That must be who you mean. Do you know where he is?"

"No, I'm sorry. I haven't seen him in a very long time. One day we were on an adventure together and we were separated by a giant whale. By the time I got to the other side, he was gone. I've never seen him again."

"I can't believe this." Michelle frowned. "Not long ago I didn't even know my grandfather went missing or that another world exists. Why would my parents lie to me about all of that?"

"I'm sure they were just trying to protect you." Bea crawled along the rock toward her. "This other world—it's nothing wonderful or magical. Its full of scary, terrible creatures."

"Are you sure?" Michelle turned to look at her. "Have you seen it?"

"Well, no, but I've heard Carlos's stories and stories from others that have seen it." She shivered. "It sounds scary enough to me. I'd prefer to stay far away from it. Don't despair, princess, Carlos and I will help you find your way back home."

"I'm not a princess." Michelle narrowed her eyes. "Not yet. And I'm not going back home. I'm going to find my grandfather. I'm sure that he will tell me the truth." Michelle swam up through the water toward the crack in the rocks. "He was brave enough to explore, maybe he will be brave enough to convince my mother and father to change some of their rules."

"What if we can't find him, Michelle?" Kira swam up beside her. "Will you come back home with us then?"

"Yes." Michelle frowned. "If I can't find him, I will go back home. I promise." She looked at her two friends. "You don't have to come with me, not if you don't want to. This is my adventure and I've already put you both in danger."

"We're going." Trina smiled as she hugged her friend.

"Absolutely." Kira nodded.

"Us too!" Bea crawled onto Trina's shoulder. "Do you mind if I hitch a ride?"

"Not at all." Trina smiled at her.

"I'll do my best to keep up!" Carlos called out from the sand.

"Here." Kira swam down to him. "You can hold onto my hair."

"I can?" He stared at her. "Are you sure?"

"Yes. I'm sure." She smiled as she looped her hair around his claws. "You saved my life, the least I can do is give you a ride."

"Thank you." He smiled at her, then settled onto her back.

As Michelle led the way out of the rocks, she was glad to have two new friends. She hoped that her adventure would lead her to her grandfather or maybe even the other world that Carlos spoke of, but she worried that it might lead them into more danger than she could imagine.

# EIGHT

"Can you take us to the last place you saw him?" Michelle looked over her shoulder at Carlos. "Do you remember where that was?"

"Yes, I know it well." He frowned. "But it is dangerous there. Large creatures roam. Creatures far larger than you."

"We'll be careful." Michelle smiled. "I'm sure we'll be fine."

"I wouldn't be so sure." Carlos spoke softly. "I think there is something I should tell you."

"Yes?" Michelle swam closer to him. He still hung from Kira's hair. "What is it?"

"When I said I'd never seen your grandfather again, I didn't make myself clear. I have looked for him for many years, Michelle. I have found no sign of him." He looked into her eyes. "I fear he might have been taken by that whale—or some other creature."

"Taken?" Kira shivered. "Do you mean killed?"

"I hate to think it." Carlos shook his head. "But he and I were good friends. I do think that if he had survived, he would have found me to let me know that he was okay."

"Maybe he couldn't." Michelle's heart pounded. "Maybe he got lost."

"Your grandfather? Lost?" Carlos chuckled. "No, that's not possible. He knew the open sea better than any creature I've ever met. I don't think he could ever be lost."

"Then he is alive somewhere and we need to help him!" Michelle balled her hands into fists. "I know he is!"

"Okay, you may be right." Carlos nodded. "I will take you there. Keep swimming this way."

They did swim. They swam for hours before they all became too tired to swim any further.

"This is a good place to stop." Bea crawled off of Trina's shoulder and onto a flat rock that jutted out over a small open space. "Carlos and I will keep watch while you rest."

"Thank you." Michelle swam under the rock and stretched out in the sand. Soon Kira and Trina nestled in beside her.

She tried to imagine what her journey would have been like if she had made it alone. She couldn't even picture it. Having her two best friends beside her made everything seem better.

But as she started to drift off to sleep, she thought of her parents. How worried were they? What about her sisters? Did they know she was gone?

She guessed that they probably did. In fact, they were probably searching everywhere for her.

She had promised her friends she would go back home if she couldn't find her grandfather, but could she? The thought of how angry everyone would be made her sick to her stomach. How could she explain why she left?

Her thoughts shifted to the other world Carlos had described. Was it possible that he was telling the truth? Could there be another place? A world full of different creatures?

The thought thrilled her. She wanted more than anything to learn about it. But first, she had a mission to complete. If her grandfather was out there somewhere all alone, she wanted to find him. Maybe he could explain to her why her parents and the rest of the mermaid world had kept so many secrets.

When she woke up, it surprised her. She hadn't realized that she'd fallen asleep. Yet she had the sense that quite a bit of time had passed. Kira and Trina were still asleep. So was Bea, curled up on Trina's shoulder. But Carlos guarded them all.

"Carlos?" She swam out to him. "Did I sleep a long time?"

"A very long time." He smiled. "You must have been tired."

"I was." She looked around in the water. "Was it quiet?"

"Yes, a little too quiet." He tipped his head toward the others. "We should wake them and be on our way."

"Why do you think it's too quiet?" She peered through the water.

"When there aren't many creatures around, there's usually a reason." He scuttled back toward the sleeping mermaids. "Let's go! Wake up, little fish!"

"Fish?" Kira woke up with a start. "Did you just call me a fish?"

"I'm sure he meant it in a nice way." Trina stretched her arms out above her head.

"How could calling me a fish be nice?" Kira crossed her arms.

"I meant no offense." Carlos laughed. "Just that you swim like fish, so I think of you as fish."

"Well I am most certainly not a fish!" Kira frowned as she swam out to join Michelle.

"We're a little bit like fish." Michelle shrugged. "We have the tails, the scales, and the gills."

"Ugh, not you too!" Kira spun through the water in a swift and fancy twirl. "Can fish do that?"

"Not any that I've seen." Carlos clacked his claws. "Very nice!"

"Thank you. So, remember, I'm a mermaid, not a fish!"

"I'll remember, but there's no time to argue! We must move on my mermaid friends—and quickly!"

"Why?" Trina looked around. "Everything looks peaceful."

"Yes, it does look peaceful, that's the problem!" He looked around quickly, then waved his claws through the water. "Hurry! We must go!"

"Oh dear, we might be too late." Bea slid up along Trina's shoulder until she reached the top of her head. "Something is casting a very big shadow.

Michelle looked up in time to see a dark shadow glide over the top of them. It was larger than any shadow she'd ever seen.

"Is that what I think it is?" Kira ducked behind Michelle.

"It might be." Trina huddled close as well. "I've heard stories about enormous sharks, but I'd hoped that they were made up to keep us close to home."

"I'm sorry to tell you that they're not just stories." Carlos grabbed onto Kira's hair. "We need to get out of here and fast. Hopefully the shark didn't spot us!"

"I'm pretty sure it did!" Trina shrieked as the water began to rumble all around them. "Swim faster! Faster!"

# NINE

Michelle's heart pounded as she swam as fast as she could. She didn't dare to look back, but she could imagine how huge and hungry the shark might be. Would he go after all of them or just one?

She realized that if she didn't do something, they might all become dinner. Maybe she wasn't ready to be a princess, but that didn't mean that it wasn't her job to protect her people.

She glanced over at each of her friends, then she suddenly changed direction.

"Keep swimming!" she shouted to them. "I'll distract the shark!"

She swam straight toward the shark, which was far larger than she'd even imagined. It made her dizzy with fear to stare at his wide mouth as he cut through the water in her direction.

"Michelle!" Trina shouted. "Get away from it!"

"It's too late!" Kira grabbed Trina's arm. "We have to keep going, it's what she wants us to do!"

"But she'll never make it!" Trina fought against Kira's grip.

"If anyone can, it's Michelle." Kira tugged her forward. "We can't let Carlos and Bea get eaten, not after Michelle has done this to protect all of us."

Michelle did her best not to think about the danger she'd put herself in. As long as her friends made it out safe, she would be happy. But the shark that barreled toward her was hard to ignore.

She ducked off to the side and tried to swim around him. As she did, she felt the ripple of the water that splashed off of his body. He moved so fast that he created his own current, a current that she found herself caught up in.

As she tumbled in the force of the water, she realized that she wouldn't be able to escape.

Just as she was ready to surrender, a shrill sound rang through her ears. It was so loud and so overpowering that she clutched at her ears in an attempt to escape it. As she twisted and covered her ears, the shark thrashed and rolled through the water.

He seemed to be just as bothered by the sound as she was. It made the water feel electrified.

Her skin prickled and her teeth chattered.

The shark lunged toward her, then sank to the sand below. He rolled there for a few seconds, then bolted off in the opposite direction.

Michelle stared after him as her ears continued to ring. She looked in the direction her friends had swum in, but they were gone. As she rubbed her ears, she realized she was safe. The shark had been scared off by the sound.

Still a little dizzy from the ringing, she sank down to the sand for a rest.

"Michelle!" Trina shouted.

"Michelle, where are you?" Kira shouted.

"I'm here!" Michelle waved her hand through the water. "The shark is gone, I'm here!"

"Oh, Michelle!" Trina swam toward her with Kira right behind. As they hugged, all three friends laughed with relief.

"How did you escape?" Carlos stared at her.

"That was the biggest shark I've ever seen." Bea crept out from under Trina's hair.

"I didn't escape." Michelle shook her head. "Something saved me. It was this sound—a sound like nothing I've ever heard before." She turned to look through the water. "I think it came from that way." She pointed toward a faint glow in the distance.

As she stared, she saw something move in the water.

"Look!" Michelle pointed to a figure ahead of them. "It's a mermaid!"

"Are you sure?" Trina tilted her head to the side. "Maybe it's just a big fish?"

"It's not a big fish!" Michelle huffed, then swam forward.

The closer she came to the figure, the more excited she became.

The mermaid, however, managed to swim just faster than her. If she noticed Michelle following her, she didn't turn back to see who it was. She had a faint glow around her and something strapped over her shoulder—something that Michelle had never seen before.

"Wait! Please!" She swam as fast as she could. "Please stop!"

The mermaid suddenly turned to face her and that's when Michelle realized that it was a merman, not a mermaid.

His long white hair flowed around his head. His eyes glowed a mixture of green and black as the deepest waters she'd ever seen. They reminded her of her mother's eyes.

"Grandfather?" She stared at him.

"You shouldn't be here." He stared back at her.

"I've been looking for you." She shook her head. "I thought you might need my help."

"You thought I might need your help?" He chuckled. "Little princess, all I need is for you to be safe."

"I'm not a princess!" Michelle crossed her arms. "Not yet at least. I wanted to explore. I didn't want to be trapped in the Coral Palace."

"Trapped in the Coral Palace? What do you mean?" He looked up as the others gathered close. "What are the three of you doing so far away from home? Carlos, is that you?"

"It's me!" Carlos waved as he hung from Kira's hair. "Good to see you again, old friend!"

"You too." The merman smiled. "I thought that whale got you."

"I thought he got *you*!" Carlos chuckled. "I'm so glad to see that he didn't."

"Was it you that saved me from that shark, Grandfather?" Michelle swam closer to him.

"It wasn't me exactly, but a special tool I was given." He patted the small square box that hung from his shoulder. "It emits a sound that the sharks don't like. It's kept me safe a few times and I'm glad I had it to keep you safe." He frowned. "This part of the sea isn't safe for you."

"I just want to have adventures and explore—like you!" She smiled. "Can't I stay with you? Please?"

"No, darling." He wrapped an arm around her. "What I am doing, you can't help me with. I've made some terrible mistakes and now I'm trying to fix them."

"Mistakes? What kind of mistakes?"

"Because of me, the human world suspects that mermaids exist. I've been trying to protect the mermaid world from being discovered ever since." He hung his head. "There isn't a day that goes by that I don't wish I had stayed in the Coral Palace."

# TEN

"Then why don't you come back with us?" Michelle took her grandfather's hand. "Mother misses you so much."

"I'm sure that she does. I'm sorry that I was never able to tell her that I'm safe. But now you can be the one to tell her." He pulled a chain of gems from around his neck.

"Take this treasure back to your mother." He handed her the string of gems. "She will know what to do with it."

"But Grandfather, I don't want to go back." She drew back from the gems. "I don't care about treasure. I want to explore. I want to see what you've seen—and more."

"Michelle, it is far too dangerous." He looked up at the water that sparkled with the sunlight that drifted down through it. It created the glow all around him. "I know it is tempting. It all looks so beautiful." He looked back at her. "But the truth is, the world up there—the world of the humans—it's a cruel and terrifying place. Our world is beautiful and peaceful and it's all we need. I made a terrible mistake by coming here, by contacting the humans, and now I have to try to fix it by keeping them away from our world. That is my job now and I have to keep doing it."

"But Grandfather—"

He lifted the string of gems and hung it around her neck. "Now your job is to get safely back home and give this to your mother. Tell her that you've seen me, tell her that I am doing my best to protect everyone." He shook his head. "Tell her that I'm sorry that I've caused this danger to spread." He looked straight into her eyes. "Whether or not you want to be a princess, little one, you are a princess. It is your job to keep the mermaid world and the Coral Palace safe. Can I count on you to do that?"

"It can't be so terrible." Michelle frowned. "I've seen a giant squid, an octopus, and an enormous shark. What could be more terrible than that?"

"It is far more terrible than any of those things." He touched her cheek. "There was a time when I believed that the human world and the mermaid world should communicate. But now I know how wrong I was. Please, promise me that you will do your best to protect our world."

"I promise." Michelle bit into her lip. She wanted to ask a million questions, but she knew that he wouldn't answer them. "I'll go back and I'll give my mother these gems."

"Good." He smiled as he looked at her. "It is good to know that there is such a brave young princess guarding the Coral Palace in my absence. And you both will help her?" He looked at Kira, then Trina.

"We will." Kira nodded. She took Michelle's hand. "It's time to go home now."

"But we can't." Michelle glanced over her shoulder. "We don't know the way."

"The gems will guide you." Her grandfather pointed to the necklace. "They will glow as you go in the right direction. Just follow their glow."

"I will." Michelle clutched the gems. "I wish I could stay with you."

"One day I will tell you of all my adventures, but right now, your most important job is to be crowned a princess, so that you can keep our family and our world safe." He touched the top of her head. "Be safe, my granddaughter, and journey home swiftly. Your journey may be coming to an end, but your adventure is just beginning."

Swimming away from her grandfather was the hardest thing Michelle ever had to do.

As she swam, the gems on the necklace glowed. If she went in the wrong direction, the glow faded until she was going in the right direction again. She was curious about how they worked and sad that she had to leave her grandfather behind. But she was very excited to tell her mother about her discovery.

When they arrived at the Coral Palace, guards rushed toward them.

"It's the princess!" one of them shouted. "She's returned!"

Soon the shout was repeated in many different voices in many different directions.

Michelle braced herself as she swam into the Coral Palace. Would her mother be angry? Had she missed her chance to be crowned?

"Michelle!" Her mother swam toward her, her arms spread wide. "Oh, Michelle! You are safe!" She looked past her at Kira and Trina. "You're all safe! What a joyous day!"

"I'm sorry, Mother, I know I shouldn't have left. But I felt I had no choice. I wanted an adventure." She lifted the gems from around her neck. "I found Grandfather and he asked me to bring these to you."

"You what?" Her mother's eyes widened. "You found him?" As she took the gems, her hands trembled. "Is he well?"

"Yes. He said that he has a job to do—to protect the mermaid world. He can't come back yet, but he said that you would know what to do with these. They aren't sea gems, are they?"

"No, they're not." Her mother stared at them. "I suppose it's time I told you the truth. Will you excuse us please, Kira and Trina? I know that your families are waiting to see you."

"Yes, of course." Trina started to back away.

"Oh, Trina dear, you have something on your shoulder!" The queen's eyes widened.

"This is Bea." Trina smiled. "A friend."

"And I'm Carlos!" The lobster swung from Kira's hair and attempted to bow slightly. "Pleasure to meet you, my queen!"

"Oh my!"

"Mother, they kept us safe and helped us on our journey. Can't they stay?" Michelle looked into her eyes.

"Of course they can. They are welcome. Now, Michelle, come with me."

Michelle took her mother's hand as she led her through the Coral Palace. They traveled down corridors that she'd never seen before, until they reached a space deep under the sand.

"Your grandfather began collecting things when he was a young merman." She pulled back thick piles of seaweed. "He knew they were not of our world. He saved them here. He hoped that one day he would be able to learn more about the human world." She looked over at Michelle. "Since his disappearance, we all thought it would be better if we never mentioned the other world. We thought it would keep you safer." She moved aside to give Michelle a view of the space.

It was filled with strange items of all shapes and sizes, things that Michelle knew didn't belong in the sea.

"Mother! I had no idea this was here." She began to swim forward.

"Don't, Michelle. It is forbidden." She let the seaweed fall back into place. "I am only showing you now, so that you can help me protect the others. Your grandfather thought the humans would want to work with us to protect the sea, but I guess that is not what happened."

"No. He said the human world was a terrible place." She frowned. "Can that really be true?"

"If he says it is, then it is as I feared." She clutched the gems tightly in her hand. "It's time for your crowning, Michelle. I hope now you know just how important it is for you to protect our world."

"I do."

Michelle followed her mother back to the throne room.

As all the mermaids gathered, including her father, sisters, and friends, she finally understood what it meant to be a princess. But she also knew that guarding the palace would never be enough for her.

As the crown was placed on her head she smiled at her friends. Now she understood that she had a job to do, that she would have to do much more to protect her world.

She thought of her grandfather and the adventures she still wanted to have and somehow she knew that one day her dreams would come true. One day, she'd see with her own eyes this other world that existed. One day, her grandfather would come back to Eldoris to live with them again in the Coral Palace.

## ALSO BY PJ RYAN

Amazon.com/author/pjryan

*Visit the author page to save big on special bundled sets!

Additional Series:

The Fairies of Sunflower Grove

The Mermaids of Eldoris

Rebekah - Girl Detective

RJ - Boy Detective

Mouse's Secret Club

Rebekah, Mouse & RJ Special Editions

Jack's Big Secret

# AVAILABLE IN AUDIO

PJ Ryan books for kids are also available as audiobooks.

Visit the author website for a complete list at: PJRyanBooks.com

You can also listen to free audio samples there.

Made in the USA
Columbia, SC
22 July 2020